| DATE | | | |
|---|---|---|---|
| | | | |
| | | | |
| | | | |
| | | | |
| | | | |
| | | | |
| | | | |
| | | | |
| | | | |
| | | | |
| | | | |
| | | | |

# Child Star

The ONCE UPON AMERICA™ Series

## A LONG WAY TO GO
*A Story of Women's Right To Vote*
by Zibby Oneal

## HERO OVER HERE
*A Story of World War I*
by Kathleen V. Kudlinski

## IT'S ONLY GOODBYE
*An Immigrant Story*
by Virginia T. Gross

## THE DAY IT RAINED FOREVER
*A Story of the Johnstown Flood*
by Virginia T. Gross

## PEARL HARBOR IS BURNING!
*A Story of World War II*
by Kathleen V. Kudlinski

## CHILD STAR
*When Talkies Came to Hollywood*
by Lydia Weaver

# Child Star

WHEN TALKIES CAME TO HOLLYWOOD

## BY LYDIA WEAVER

ILLUSTRATED BY MICHELE LAPORTE

VIKING

VIKING
Published by the Penguin Group
Viking Penguin, a division of Penguin Books USA Inc.,
375 Hudson Street, New York, New York 10014, U.S.A.
Penguin Books Ltd, 27 Wrights Lane, London W8 5TZ, England
Penguin Books Australia Ltd, Ringwood, Victoria, Australia
Penguin Books Canada Ltd, 10 Alcorn Avenue, Toronto,
Ontario, Canada M4V 3B2
Penguin Books (N.Z.) Ltd, 182–190 Wairau Road,
Auckland 10, New Zealand

Penguin Books Ltd, Registered Offices: Harmondsworth,
Middlesex, England

First published in 1992 by Viking Penguin, a division of
Penguin Books USA Inc.

1   3   5   7   9   10   8   6   4   2

Library of Congress Cataloging-in-Publication Data
Weaver, Lydia.
Child star : when talkies came to Hollywood / by Lydia Weaver ;
illustrated by Michele Laporte.
p.      cm. — (Once upon America)
Summary: Ten-year-old Little Joey Norman, a hot new star in the
silent films of Hollywood, wonders if he can make the transition to
the talkies when sound is introduced to the movies.
ISBN 0-670-84039-4
[1. Motion pictures—Fiction. ˙ 2. Hollywood (Los Angeles, Calif.)—
Fiction.]   I. Laporte, Michele, ill.   II. Title.   III. Series.
PZ7.W3585Ch   1992
[Fic]—dc20   91-29847   CIP   AC

Printed in the U.S.A.
Set in 12 point Goudy Oldstyle

*For Bruce, of course*

# Contents

# Such a Dreamer

Joey was dreaming about Babe Ruth. In his dream, the Babe was asking Joey's advice. "I've been striking out a lot, kiddo," he said, flexing his huge hands around the neck of his bat. "I'm not sure what to do about it. I just don't know what I'm going to do." And then the Babe started to cry.

Joey woke up and laughed aloud. Babe Ruth crying! But then he heard his mother in the kitchen with Mrs. Ogilvie, their landlady. Mama was crying and saying, "I just don't know what to do."

Joey slipped out of bed and tiptoed to the door, listening. "Since Jack died, I've had to take whatever job I could get to scrape us by. I have no skills or talents except the piano. Nobody has the money for lessons these days . . ."

Money again! Mama was always talking about money. "President Coolidge says 1927 is the age of prosperity. That means everybody has a chance to make lots of money," she once told him. "But it isn't working. The only ones making money are already rich. It isn't fair, Joey."

Joey pulled on his knickers. The brown wool was scratchy and hot. He wished he could have light tan poplin ones like Freddy Hokiyama downstairs. But Joey knew he shouldn't complain. His brown wool suit had cost $14.75 at Boos Brothers. It came with two pairs of knickers—"One pair for play, one pair for good," Mama said, "and they'll have to last you the year."

As he was buttoning his shirt, Joey heard his own name from the kitchen. "And what about Joey? It was fine when he was in school, but it's summer now. He's such a dreamer. No telling the trouble that boy could get into alone here all day."

Joey wanted to shout, "I'm ten years old! I can take care of myself!"

Before he could, Mrs. Ogilvie said, "Well, Helen, he could come with me to the Angelus."

Joey froze. Once before, he'd had to go with Mrs. Ogilvie to the big church on Glendale Boulevard. He'd had to sit still all day, listening to the great Mrs. Aimee Semple McPherson preach about the devil who made his home in Hollywood. For a minute, Joey had been interested: where in Hollywood did the devil live? Maybe the big white house with the iron gates on Mapleton Drive? But no, he remembered that Mama had told him that was the home of a famous movie star.

The worst part of the long day was the dime Mrs. Ogilvie had given him. She made him put it into the plate the usher passed around for the church fund. In his mind, Joey could see the silver plate filled with all the jawbreakers and sour balls and chocolate babies ten cents could buy.

"Thank you anyway, Mrs. Ogilvie," he heard Mama say now, "but you're so busy, I couldn't ask you. Maybe the Hokiyamas again . . ."

Joey breathed a sigh of relief. Hooray for Mama! The Hokiyamas were a different story. They were a Japanese family who lived downstairs. Freddy Hokiyama was Joey's best friend.

"No, the baby's sick," Mrs. Ogilvie said.

Joey pulled open the door. His mother and Mrs. Ogilvie were sitting at the kitchen table. Joey saw Mama quickly wipe her eyes with her hankie.

"Joey, darling!" Mrs. Ogilvie cried. "How's my

angel boy?" She hurried over and hugged him.

Joey tried to pull away, but she only tightened her iron grip. She kissed him on top of his head and ruffled his hair. "Just look at these golden curls! And he's small for his age. Oh, what a beauty he'd be if he were a girl!"

Joey managed to duck out of her embrace and went over to stand behind his mother's chair, scowling. "Can't you say good morning, sleepyhead?" Mama said, catching his eye and giving him a wink.

"Morning," Joey muttered.

"I've been thinking, Joey," Mama said. "How would you like it if I took you to the studio with me today?"

Joey looked at her. He'd begged her for months to take him to the studio. It seemed like a magic place to him. It was where movies were made!

"Really?"

"Really! So hurry and go scrub behind your ears, mister. Why, I believe you could grow radishes in the dirt back there!"

Soon, Joey and Mama were walking in the June sunshine down Figueroa Street. Palm trees swayed above them in the orange-scented air, and dust blew around them as a noisy motorcar drove by.

"It's an Oldsmobile," Joey announced. "I'd like to have a Nash. They can go 40 miles per hour!"

"Why settle for a Nash?" Mama teased. "Why not buy a custom-made Luxury Phaeton?"

Joey grinned. "After I buy the motorcar for me, I'm going to buy you a big house, Mama. High on a hill, so you can see the ocean. And a new piano, a white one, with your name written on it in gold!"

Mama sighed. "Joey, Joey. How did you get to be such a dreamer?"

# Knights, Kings, Gorillas, and Indians

Hollywood Boulevard was crowded with people and motorcars and streetcars, all wanting to go somewhere in a hurry. A block away, Joey could see the tall white gates of World Studios.

Many people were standing in front of the gates. High above their heads, on top of a pole, was a huge gold globe of the earth, for "World" Studios, Mama explained.

She looked worried when she saw the crowd. "World can always use extras, but not all these folks. Oh, there are so many people who need work."

"Are you an extra, Mama?"

"I'll do whatever they want. Sometimes I sit at a table in one of their make-believe restaurants. Or maybe I'll be in the background walking down a street. Usually I just play the piano. Well, come on."

She took his hand and pushed through to the front. A sweaty, nasty-looking man was sending people, one at a time, through a door on one side of the gates.

Joey was silent. Every day his mother put on her best dress, coat, and hat and set out for "work." For the first time, Joey realized that Mama never knew if there would be a job waiting for her or not. The sweaty man had to look her over first, to decide if she was needed. If she was, she got two dollars for the day and a box lunch.

Joey felt himself growing warm. He didn't like the way the man pointed at some people and waved others away. He wished Mama was a seamstress like Mrs. Hokiyama, or a landlady, like Mrs. Ogilvie.

Joey put his arms around his mother from behind and hugged her hard, remembering the big house with the view of the ocean that he'd promised her. *Someday*, he thought . . .

"Joey—Joey, dear, let go, sweetheart." Mama's

voice sounded funny, and Joey looked up to see the sweaty man staring down at him.

"The kid with you?" the man snapped. At Mama's nod, he said, "*Umbrella* needs a piano. Go on. But keep the brat out of trouble—and he has to share your lunch."

"Yes, sir!" Mama pulled Joey along behind her.

On the way past, Joey stuck his tongue out and stepped hard on the man's foot. The man yelled, "Hey!" But Mama yanked Joey around the corner and out of his sight.

Inside the gates, it was as if they were in another city. Next to Joey and Mama were several big brick buildings, all with the World Studios globe painted on the sides. Beyond the buildings were streets with real street signs. Somebody pushed past them. When Joey looked up he gasped aloud. It was a very tall Indian! He wore a long, feathered warbonnet, red and black war paint on his face, and he had a scary-looking tomahawk hanging from his belt.

The giant Indian glanced down at Joey and growled, "What are you looking at, kid?" Joey noticed that he had an Old Gold cigarette dangling from his lower lip.

"Come along," Mama said, taking Joey's hand. She whispered in his ear as she led him away, "That man is an actor, Joey. He's in one of the motion

pictures. You'll see lots of strange sights before the day is over."

Joey looked back. The Indian was leaning against the wall, talking to a man in a gorilla suit. The man held the gorilla head, his own head sticking out of the hairy suit like a pale balloon.

Mama continued, "Today I'll be playing the piano on the set of the picture *Let a Smile Be Your Umbrella.* Mavis MacNeil is the star, and Hubert Delacroix is her leading man. He's so handsome, and she . . . well, she is the cat's meow. You've never seen anyone so beautiful."

"Why do you have to play the piano, Mama?"

"Sometimes it helps the actors to hear music when they're acting a scene. It gets them in the mood, I guess. Also, there's an awful lot of noise around them—people yelling, cameras whirring, carpenters hammering. The movies may be silent, but a movie studio is the loudest place I've ever been."

Joey didn't know where to look first. A man dressed like a king walked past, looking hot in his fur-trimmed cape and heavy crown. Three knights wearing suits of armor galloped by on horseback. They were followed by a group of beautiful ladies wearing short sparkly skirts and high heels.

And then, down at the end of one long street, Joey saw an entire dusty Western town. He was amazed. He recognized it from a motion picture he

11

and Freddy had just seen. Breaking away from his mother, ignoring her calls, he ran down the Western street, unable to believe his eyes. The bad cowboy had burst in the door of the saloon, busting up a poker fight with guns blazing. Joey climbed the steps of the saloon and pushed through the doors.

Blinking, he stood in the sun on the other side. Long pieces of wood propped up the flat front of the saloon. There was no inside! It was *just* a front. But he'd seen the men playing poker, he'd seen the bar, he'd seen the mirror shatter when the bullets hit it. What happened to it all?

A voice said, "M-m-m-magic, eh, sonny?"

Joey looked up. A big fat man dressed like a hobo, dirt smudged on his face, a battered bowler hat on his head, leaned against the fake wall a few feet away. "Fozzy Dixon!" Joey exclaimed in delight. Fozzy Dixon was the funniest man in the world. Joey and Mama had seen all his films, laughing until they cried.

"Right you are. B-b-b-bright boy." Fozzy Dixon had a stutter, Joey noticed. One letter would cause him to trip up until he forced the word out. It didn't seem to bother him much, though.

Fozzy held out a stick of Blatz Grape Gum, and Joey took it. He thought Fozzy looked even bigger and fatter in real life than he did on the movie screen. "Want to see some more m-m-magic?" Fozzy asked. He stuck his thumb in his mouth and blew hard on it. As he blew, his round face reddening with effort, the bowler hat slowly rose a few inches off his forehead.

"How'd you do that?" Joey looked closely at Fozzy's fleshy thumb.

"Trick of the t-trade. But seeing as I like you, I'll let you in on it." Fozzy showed Joey how he pressed the back brim of the hat against the wall behind him, which raised the front brim. At the same time, he blew on his thumb. The hat looked like it was rising on a puff of air. "You try it," he offered.

Joey soon got the hang of it. "Not bad at all," Fozzy said. "You got a mama or a papa nearby, k-k-kid?"

"A mama. My father died nine years ago. My mama plays the piano on *Let a Smile Be Your Umbrella*."

"Say, I'm in that."

"You are? Gee, swell! I thought it was all mushy love stuff."

"Now that you mention it," Fozzy said, "that spoiled Mavis and her loverboy *are* kind of hogging the c-c-camera, and pushing old Fozzy aside."

"You should go right up to her and say, 'Hey, you Dumb Dora, scram! This is my show!' "

Fozzy laughed, a cheerful, rumbling sound. Then he looked hard at Joey. "Lately, I've been thinking I need a sidekick to liven things up on this picture.

Even the odds, so to speak."

"Like that dog in your last one?"

"Nah, that mutt was a scene-stealer. Oh, I don't know. It's just a thought. Say, k-kid, you're all right. You caught on to that hat trick awful fast."

Joey blew a big bubble of Blatz Grape Gum. Fozzy leaned over and popped it with his finger, and they both laughed.

# "Let a Smile
Be Your
Umbrella"

After they'd talked for a while, Fozzy said, "Let's go find your mama, p-pal."

He led Joey down another street. They passed a platform, 30 feet high, where a herd of sheep calmly grazed on grass and shrubbery. Joey stared up at them.

Fozzy laughed. "They need a long shot through that window. They tried it down on the ground, but the sheep kept wandering off. Up there, they stay put."

15

Around the next corner, they came to a big white building. Fozzy opened a door and they stepped into a huge dark room. A crowd of people stood at one end of the room among a forest of tall poles. Bright, hissing lights hung on the ends of the poles like the droopy heads of giant sunflowers.

A big camera and all the lights were aimed at what looked like the living room of a very fancy house. It had red carpets, velvet curtains, and a sweeping staircase leading up to . . . to nothing. There was no roof, no upper floor. Just the bright room in the corner of the bigger room, and a crowd of people standing around on the edges peering in.

Just then, Joey saw his mother seated at a piano in the darkness off to the side. "Mama!" he called. All the people at that end of the room turned.

A man with a big megaphone and an angry face broke away from the others and came toward them. Mama hurried timidly at his heels. "Fozzy Dixon!" the man cried. "Where've you been? You're in this scene!"

"Now, don't have k-k-kittens, McFee," Fozzy said. "You're gonna thank me for this."

"For what?"

"For saving this picture."

"And how, pray tell, are you going to do that?"

"My friend, I'd like to introduce you to the next Hollywood sensation. Little Joey Norman, t-t-take a bow." Mama gasped. Joey's mouth fell open. The man's face flushed purple.

Joey took a step backward. He thought the man was going to burst out of his skin with rage. Just then, a lady in a shimmering silver gown glided out from behind Mama.

"Oh, he's just the bee's knees, Fozzy darling! Wherever did you find him? Oh, that hair. Oh, little man, you are adorable." She took Joey's hand in her cool fingers. A cloud of perfume swirled around him. He felt dizzy.

Then the lady turned to the angry man. "I never thought I'd say this, Henry, but I'm with Fozzy. We must have this child."

And that's when everything began to happen very fast. Mr. McFee, who turned out to be the director, talked for a long time to Mama. She kept nodding in a dazed way.

Several men with tan, buttery skin and hair like patent leather arrived. They eyed Joey as Mavis MacNeil, the beautiful lady in silver, talked to them in a low voice. Finally, Joey was whisked off to a place called "Wardrobe," a room with a thousand costumes hanging in rows: soldiers' uniforms, cowboy suits, armor, long silk robes.

The wardrobe man looked at Joey. "You're supposed to be a poor homeless stray, eh?" he said. "Orphaned street kid? Well, what you got on looks perfect to me. We'll just give you a cap." He slapped a porkpie hat on Joey's head and sent him out the door. Joey didn't have a chance to protest that these were his good knickers from Boos Brothers.

Then a lady with a sour frown rubbed some greasy black stuff all over his face. Before he knew it, Joey was standing with Fozzy at a window on the other side of the bright living room. He caught a glimpse of Mama's pale face at the piano. She looked as if she couldn't believe what was happening.

Mr. McFee said, "All right, my boy. You and Fozzy are going to rob this house. You're going to open the window carefully and climb in. You'll look around to make sure no one's home. Then you'll wave Fozzy in after you. Got that?"

"That's what motion pictures are, kid," Fozzy whispered, seeing Joey's surprise. "We make them up as we go along. This is no stage p-p-play with lines to learn. You'll be fine."

Mr. McFee barked, "Piano. I want it stormy. Dark." Mama began to play, her fingers running up and down the keyboard. "Rain and wind men! Go!"

Joey heard a whirring noise and felt something wet. He looked up. Above him on a platform stood a man spraying a hose on him and Fozzy. Next to the man was a giant fan that blew the water in gusts so it battered against the windowpane.

"Camera rolling," called Mr. McFee. "Action!"

Gently, Fozzy pushed Joey, who was wiping water out of his eyes. "Boy!" screamed the director. "Open the window!"

Joey did as he was told. He climbed through the window and stood in the glare of the hottest, brightest lights this side of the sun. Somehow, with Mr. McFee shouting instructions at him from behind the bright lights, and Fozzy cheering him on, he got through the scene. Mostly it was the sight of Mama's beaming face at the piano that kept him going.

"Mavis!" yelled Mr. McFee. "Now!"

Joey had been told to go through drawers in one of the cabinets. Now, out of the corner of his eye, he saw a door open at the back of the room. He saw the shimmering silver dress. He turned toward Mavis, not knowing what to expect. She looked at him, her eyes grew wide, and her hands flew to her throat. He started to smile nervously.

"Okay, Mavis, let it rip," said Mr. McFee.

And Mavis screamed, the longest, loudest scream Joey had ever heard. He stood trapped in the sound, until Mr. McFee called, "Cut! We got it!"

Suddenly everyone was clapping. Fozzy was shaking Joey's hand. Mavis kissed him. And Mama was laughing and crying at the same time.

# An Actor's Life

A summer had never gone so fast. Last summer, Joey had spent long, lazy days playing marbles with Freddy Hokiyama. Sometimes they looked for snakes in the orange groves beyond the highway.

Now, every morning, Mama woke Joey up when it was still dark. They were driven in a Ford Model T to World Studios by a man in a red uniform. Joey knew he should be excited, but he was too sleepy.

Once at the studio, he would have more black dirt rubbed on his face and dust thrown on his old

Boos Brothers knickers. He had all brand-new clothes now: some sharp new suits and shirts, and three pairs of tan poplin pants like Freddy Hokiyama's.

Joey never had time to see Freddy anymore and missed him very much. Still, he knew he'd found a new best friend in Fozzy Dixon.

Fozzy seemed like another kid to Joey. All day long on the set, he'd play pranks on people. Joey was an eager student. "Take Mavis some t-t-t-tea," Fozzy would whisper.

So Joey would get Mavis's china cup with the tiny rosebuds on it. He'd fill it up with tea, and carry it to where she was sitting. At the last second, he'd pretend to trip, catching his foot on his other leg just the way Fozzy had shown him. He'd fly up in the air, bobbling the teacup dangerously. Mavis would scream as Joey fell to the ground, and then he would get to his feet smiling. He'd hold out the unbroken teacup, which was still full of hot tea. Mavis would always give him a hug, but Joey could tell she didn't like Fozzy.

Neither did Mr. McFee. Once he left his megaphone sitting on the ground. Fozzy pretended to step in it by mistake, then limped around with it stuck on his foot, like a peg-leg pirate. Mr. McFee was steaming mad.

Another time, Hubert Delacroix, the leading

man, blamed Fozzy for a trick Joey had played on him. Joey had seen Hubert's fake mustache lying on the makeup table, and had sprinkled pepper on it. Later, during their big mushy kissing scene, neither Hubert nor Mavis could stop sneezing. Joey laughed and laughed. He stopped laughing when Hubert pointed at Fozzy and said, "Your days are numbered, Dixon. Just wait. Talkies are around the corner and you'll be finished."

"What did he mean?" Joey wanted to know.

Fozzy said, "Ah, it's all applesauce. Rumor says, over at Warner Brothers, they're making a p-p-picture where you can hear people talk. And me with my stutter . . . well. But I say it's bunk. Even if it's t-t-true, it'll never take. Who wants to hear people talk in movies? You hear it all day on the street. Nah, it'll never happen."

"I'm sorry about the pepper, Fozzy."

"Hey, it was a k-k-k-keen stunt. Wish I'd thought of it!"

One day, one of the men with the patent-leather hair came up to Mama and said, "We're tickled pink with Joey's work, Mrs. Norman. We'd like to sign him to a three-year contract at World. As soon as this picture comes out, he's going to be a big, big star, you'll see."

"Oh, my," said Mama.

"The only thing is," the man went on, "we're

going to have to do a little publicity, see? Slip some info to *Photoplay* and the other rags. The boys at the top think ten's too old. So we're going to say the kid's seven."

Seven? Joey was outraged. Seven was a baby! Why, he was ten years old and proud of it. He was hurt when Mama only said, "Whatever you think best, Mr. Applegate."

Joey went to Fozzy, who surprised him by saying, "Get used to it, k-k-kid. They tell *Photoplay* you're a French prince, you'd better be prepared to parlay-voo."

Joey began to see that acting wasn't quite as easy as he'd thought it would be. In fact, it was downright hard work. He was nervous about doing it right. Mr. McFee's yelling rattled him so badly that sometimes he botched it up.

When he wasn't in a scene, Joey wandered around World Studios' back lot. He remembered the first day he'd been there—it seemed so long ago! How magical it had all been. He remembered the Western street, the sheep 30 feet in the air, the big Indian.

Now he saw it through different eyes. Once, three elephants were led past him for a circus picture shooting nearby. All Joey saw were three tired animals, bleary-eyed and weary from being made to do their tricks too many times.

It was almost August. In another month school

would start. Joey wasn't going, of course. One day a man appeared on the set. Mama introduced him as "Mr. Jennings, your tutor." It was easy to duck him, though, and no one much cared. Mr. Jennings himself spent most of his time looking moony-eyed at Mavis.

As *Let a Smile Be Your Umbrella* neared the end of shooting, the mood on the set changed. No one laughed anymore. Even Fozzy seemed nervous. Joey asked him what was going on.

"T-t-talkies," he said grimly. "Everyone's scared they'll be out of a job."

"But you said it was bunk!"

"Say, kid, my dogs are k-k-killing me. I'm gonna go lie down." Fozzy went into his dressing room and shut the door.

Later, when Joey walked by, he heard Fozzy inside, saying the alphabet out loud. "A, B, C, D-D-D . . . ah, phooey!" And he started over. Joey realized Fozzy was trying to cure himself of his stammer.

Everyone was acting funny. Once, the sour-looking makeup lady whispered in Joey's ear, "You're a very lucky boy. Don't you forget it. So many people in this country have no work at all." There was a sound in her voice that made Joey squirm. Was she angry at him?

He knew he was lucky. World Studios had found

him and Mama a house in the Santa Monica hills. Soon he'd buy Mama a new piano. And he'd heard that Mavis owned a private railroad car on the Twentieth Century Limited. She could ride around the country in her own train! That sounded great to Joey. He wanted one, too.

Then he wondered where he'd ever find the time to enjoy his own railroad car.

Yes, he was very lucky. But he was also working very hard.

# "Little Joey Norman"

"Listen, Joey. I have some terrible news. There's been a mudslide. The apartment building where you used to live? Well, it's been buried." Mr. McFee's face was grave. "And . . . I'm afraid your little friend Freddy Hokiyama went with it."

Joey tried to take in what he was saying. Freddy—buried in a mudslide? The hot lights blinded him, the porkpie hat itched his scalp as he struggled to speak. His best friend, Freddy . . . dead?

"Yes, dead, Joey. I'm afraid you'll never see him again."

Tears stung Joey's eyes. "Freddy!" he cried, looking around for Mama. He saw her behind Mr. McFee, her head down and her hands over her eyes. Was she crying, too? But the hissing lights were too bright. He couldn't see clearly. He couldn't think. He began to weep.

"Cut!" called Mr. McFee happily.

The lights went off suddenly, leaving Joey sobbing on the dark set. Mama rushed toward him and took him in her arms. "Oh, Joey," she said, "it isn't true. Freddy's fine. There was no mudslide. It was for the scene. Oh, Joey . . . they wanted you to cry . . ."

When Joey finally understood that Freddy was alive, he still couldn't stop crying. Why had they told him such a terrible lie? He was an actor, wasn't he? He could have *pretended* to cry!

Mama took him home early that day. It felt strange to be entering their big new house in the middle of the afternoon. When Joey saw the blue ocean sparkling in the distance, he realized he had never once been here in the daylight.

Daylight or no, Mama put him to bed and brought him a cup of hot Ovaltine. "I'm so sorry about what happened," she said. "I told myself we were doing all this for your future. But maybe it's time for you to stop being Little Joey Norman and go back to being just Joey."

"I like being Little Joey Norman," Joey said, his

eyes beginning to close. The afternoon sun streamed in the windows. Soon he fell fast asleep and dreamed about running through the orange groves with Freddy Hokiyama, free as a bird.

Freddy Hokiyama's father was now the gardener at Joey's new house, and the next day he brought Freddy over. Joey was so glad to see him. The mudslide story had scared him.

He was eager for news of school and the outside world. To himself he thought of anything away from World Studios as the "outside World." He wanted to talk about Babe Ruth's home run record, or the big Dempsey-Tunney fight. But Freddy wanted to know what it was like to be a movie star.

"It's not that great," Joey said. "Maybe I'll quit." He remembered what Mama had said about going back to being just Joey.

But Freddy said bluntly, "You can't quit. That would mean my father would lose his job, and we would have no money." Joey looked around at the big house, and at Freddy, and realized how many people were depending on him.

Finally *Umbrella* was finished. Joey's work didn't end, though. While *Umbrella* was being edited, World was trying to find a new picture for him. His days were filled with interviews and photo sessions.

"World is grooming you to be their next big star.

How do you feel about that?" a lady interviewer asked him.

"Dogs get groomed, not boys," Joey said. One of the men with patent-leather hair shook him hard by the shoulder and scolded him for being rude.

Joey's picture appeared on the cover of *Photoplay*. Joey was disgusted to see a tear on his cheek. *Seven-Year-Old Star*, read the caption, making him even more angry.

He called Fozzy on the telephone, thinking Fozzy would understand. But Fozzy just sighed and said, "Hey, I'd do back flips, c-c-crying and whistling 'Dixie,' if it'd get me on that c-c-cover."

At the end of September, *Let a Smile Be Your Umbrella* had its world premiere at Grauman's Chinese Theater in Hollywood. World Studios sent a black Cadillac for Joey and Mama.

They picked up Fozzy along the way. Fozzy lived alone in a big house on Summit Drive in Beverly Hills. He came out to the car looking rumpled and smelling funny.

"Fozzy!" Mama said. "Have you been drinking?"

"Ssshhh," Fozzy whispered in a blurry way, "there's a law against it. P-P-Prohibition, y'know."

"I *know*," Mama said sternly.

Fozzy looked ashamed. "I'm sorry, Mrs. Norman. Only, this is the kid's first p-p-premiere . . . and I think it might be my last. I needed a shot of the giggle water, Mrs. Norman. To give me c-courage."

The driver turned right onto Hollywood Boulevard. All of a sudden, they were in the middle of a huge crowd. Police barricades kept the street clear. The big Cadillac moved slowly toward the theater. Huge spotlights swept the night sky.

"All these people," Mama breathed.

"Fans," Fozzy said. "The movies are their escape, you know. They want dreams, so they watch us on the b-b-big screen and forget for two hours they got no job. Joey here gives them hope for the future."

Joey stared out the window at the eager faces staring back in. So these people were depending on him, too.

When they got out of the car, flashbulbs popped in their eyes. The crowd seemed to swell toward them over the barricades. Joey was scared, but Fozzy gave a graceful bow, sweeping his hat in a circle. At the last moment, he fell over on his nose!

Joey knew he'd done it on purpose—it was one of his old tricks. A wave of laughter broke over them as Fozzy got to his feet. "Fozzy! Fozzy!" screamed the crowd.

He turned to Joey and Mama and muttered, "Maybe I ain't finished, after all. They still love me!" Joey was startled to see tears in his eyes.

Inside the theater, Joey saw Mavis and Hubert and Mr. McFee, and all the men with patent-leather

hair. He saw other glamorous movie stars like Doug-
las Fairbanks and Mary Pickford.

Then the lights went down and the music
started—a whole orchestra sat on the stage. *World*

*Studios Presents*, read the screen, and then Mavis's name came on. Then the title, and all of a sudden Joey read: *And Introducing: Little Joey Norman.* Mama squeezed his hand.

The picture started. There was Mavis in the living room, only you couldn't tell it had no roof, or that the staircase led nowhere. Rain poured down outside the window, but you couldn't see the man with the hose, or the fan. Mavis left the room and the window slowly opened.

Suddenly Joey had the shock of his life. Who was that little shrimp climbing in the window? The boy with the dumb-looking hat on his head? That kid with the stupid, dazed look on his dirty face, his mouth hanging slightly open . . . that couldn't be *him*, could it?

Beside him in the dark, Fozzy laughed his great, rumbling laugh. He leaned over and whispered in Joey's ear, "The first time you see yourself is the hardest, k-k-kid. But I was right about you . . . you're a star!"

# "You Ain't Heard Nothin' Yet"

Fozzy wore an overcoat and hat. The clothes were far too heavy for the Indian summer afternoon, but perfect as a disguise, he said. He even carried a silver-tipped cane and pretended to limp, as added insurance.

"Don't want some c-c-crazy fan spotting me and making a fuss," Fozzy said. But no one did and they stood in line like everyone else to pay their 10 cents and get their tickets.

The Melrose Theater was packed with people, all

of them buzzing about this new "talking picture."
Fozzy and Joey sat silently among them, hunched
down in their seats.

The Jazz Singer had had its premiere a week ago.
Since then, it was all anyone could talk about. Fozzy
and Joey had decided to see what all the fuss was
about.

The lights went down and the titles came up.
Joey noticed Fozzy unscrewing the top of his cane
and tilting it toward his mouth. "Fozzy, are you
drinking out of your cane?" he asked in wonder.

"Ssshhh. It's hollow—made for me special by a
g-g-guy I know. You don't expect me to sit through
this sober, do you?"

The picture started out silent, except for the
music, with titles to read just as always. Partway
through, Al Jolson, the star, got up on a stage and
started to sing—and you could hear his voice!

"Bunk!" muttered Fozzy.

But then Al Jolson looked straight into the camera and said, right out loud, "Wait a minute, folks.
You ain't heard nothin' yet!" He seemed to say it
directly to them.

The people in the audience around Joey and Fozzy
gasped. Then someone started to clap. Soon everyone in the theater was cheering. Sound had come
to motion pictures.

Joey was beginning to think it was all pretty swell,

in spite of himself. But Fozzy leaned over and said, "Let's scram, k-k-k-kiddo. This is giving me the heebie j-j-jeebies." His stutter seemed worse than usual.

Outside the theater, they stood blinking in the sun. Another crowd was lining up for the next showing. All of a sudden, a lady screamed, "It's Little Joey Norman!" Joey turned and saw a mob of people bearing down on him.

"Oh, isn't he adorable?" "He's cuter than his photos, look at his blond hair!" "Oooh, don't you just want to eat him up, he's a doll!" One woman grabbed his jacket. Another fingered his hair. He stepped back, trying to get away from them, but they loomed over him, closer and closer, and he started to panic. He was trapped!

A strong hand took his shoulder. "This way, k-k-kid." Fozzy pushed some people aside with his cane, and swung Joey up on a streetcar that was just pulling away from the curb.

"Phew! You all right?" he asked, climbing up after him. Joey's jacket was torn, and his hair flew every which way. "Guess you need a disguise, too, k-k-kid." Neither of them mentioned that nobody had noticed Fozzy.

"I remember the first t-time I knew my life was going to be different from any other kid's," Fozzy said as the old streetcar rattled along. "I was eight, playing vaudeville every night. It was Christmas, and my dear old mum took me to see Santa C-C-Claus. Boy, was I excited! So I get up to the old guy—he was all dressed in his red suit, with a big white b-beard and a red nose, and I'm thinking 'Holy moly—me and Santy Claus!' And then—do you believe it?—fatso looks down at me and says, 'Baby Fozzy! Can I have your autograph?' " Fozzy shook his head, chuckling.

"Yep, you grow up fast in this business," he went on. "Maybe I didn't do you no favor, kid, making you a star."

"Baby Fozzy . . ." Joey murmured.

"I'm not sorry I did it, mind you," Fozzy said. "You're making your money and saving it for a rainy day. The way things are going in this country I think we're all headed for a rainy day—a big one. Too many p-p-poor people, too many rich, not enough in between."

Joey had never heard Fozzy sound so serious. He didn't know how to answer. But then Fozzy turned to him and winked. "All this yapping's making me mighty hungry. I know a place nearby where we can get ourselves the biggest ice c-cream sundae in the state of C-California. Cherries, nuts, the works! What do you say, pal?"

Two weeks later, Joey was on his way back to World Studios. Mama sat with him in the backseat of the studio's Ford Model T. She held his hand as they went over what he would say during his voice test. They had decided on some old nursery rhymes Mama used to read him when he was a baby.

Mama coached him. "Be a little more excited when you say it, Joey. The *cow* jumped over the *moon!*"

"Aw, nerts," said Joey.

"Afterward, I'll take you out for lunch—anywhere you want, how do you like that?"

Joey had been too scared to eat breakfast. Now, as the motorcar drove through the World Studios gate, the thought of lunch made him feel sick. What if his voice was wrong for talking pictures, too squeaky, not loud enough? Everyone else's fears were catching. He was afraid he would lose his job.

Inside the studio, Joey met the head sound engineer, a man named Mr. Loud. Joey would have found his name funny, if he hadn't been so nervous.

Mr. Loud put earphones on, frowning, and twirled several of the hundreds of dials on the big black box in front of him. There were two assistants who also wore earphones. They showed Joey to a stool in the middle of a large, glassed-in booth. A microphone taller than he was stood in front of him.

"All right. Say something." Mr. Loud waved his hand at Joey, not looking at him.

Staring at the microphone as if it might bite him, Joey cleared his throat.

"Don't *do* that. These machines pick up everything, make it sound like thunder. Just talk, son."

"Hey, diddle diddle—"

"Can't hear you!"

"*Hey diddle diddle* . . ." Joey paused.

"Go on! What are you waiting for?"

"The cat and the fiddle, the *cow* jumped over the *moon* . . ." Joey got through the whole nursery rhyme and was about to start on another when he saw one of the assistants laughing. He fell silent. All his fears had come true: his voice was ridiculous.

Mr. Loud glanced up. "Okay, son. Fine. You did fine."

Fine?

"Yes, talking pictures will be perfectly all right for you. At least until your voice changes. Congratulations."

"Then why were you laughing?" Joey managed to get out.

"What? Oh . . . well, are you hungry or something, son? Because the microphone picked up your stomach growling. Loud and clear!"

# Finding a Voice

The silence balloon floated high above World Studios, a tiny speck in the blue sky. Joey sat outside trying to learn his lines, but he couldn't stop looking at the balloon. It was raised so airplanes would know a movie was shooting below and avoid the area. Otherwise, the microphones would pick up the sound of their engines.

All Joey could think was how he'd like to be a bird flying as high as the balloon. He'd like to be high above Hollywood, high above World Studios, and especially, high above the set of *The Littlest Pirate.*

Everything was different now. Learning lines was much harder than homework had ever been. And Joey was the star of the film—the whole picture rested on his shoulders. No Mavis, no Hubert . . . and saddest of all, no Fozzy.

Fozzy had failed his voice test, and World Studios had fired him. He had gone to New York, saying, "Heck, if I c-can't be in movies, I'll return to the stage! I was a star there once and I will be again."

He had sounded brave, but he'd smelled of liquor. Joey was worried about him. He'd tried to get Fozzy a part in *The Littlest Pirate,* the way Fozzy had for him in *Umbrella.* Maybe he could play a deaf-mute, or someone who didn't have to speak. But movies had scripts now. You couldn't just add a character and make up the story as you went along, and Fozzy was turned down.

Before he left he'd said, "Save your dough, and when the time comes, do something sensible, like be a plumber. The world always needs plumbers." And he had made a gurgling noise like a backed-up sink and then—*whoosh*—a flushing toilet. Even though Joey had been fighting back tears, he had to laugh . . . that was Fozzy for you.

He missed Fozzy. He missed Freddy Hokiyama. It seemed his life consisted of 18-hour days that went by so fast he hardly had time to blink.

On silent movies, the set had been noisy with people talking and laughing. Now that there was sound, the sets were deathly quiet. You had to tiptoe around in stocking feet. The Klieg lights hissed too loudly, so they'd been replaced. The cameras were all encased in heavy soundproof boxes so the microphones wouldn't hear their whirring. Certainly there was no one like Mama playing the piano to get the actors in the mood.

Mr. Loud, the sound man, was the person in charge now, not the director. Even if a scene had gone well, Mr. Loud could say, "Didn't hear him. Do it over." They had to obey.

The microphone ruled everything. "King Mike," people called it. Some of the older actors were scared of it. They would let their eyes stray to it during a scene. "You looked!" the director would cry angrily. The actors' fear began to be known as "mike fright."

Once it had been fun—pranks, laughter, Fozzy limping around with the megaphone on his foot . . .

Someone touched Joey's shoulder. His eyes flew open. Had he been asleep? The script had fallen from his hands and lay on the ground, pages fluttering in the breeze.

He looked up to see Mama standing above him. She was with a mean-looking lady dressed in dark blue, so different from the glamorous, colorful cos-

tumes everyone else wore. "I'm Mrs. Stenn," the lady announced.

"Your new tutor," Mama added.

"This boy is dead tired! How can he be expected to study his lessons?"

"Well . . ." said Mama helplessly.

Mrs. Stenn shook her head. It was terrible the way child stars had been used, she said. Expected to carry the whole picture, make money for the studio, but to have no rights at all.

"Someday, laws will be passed," she said. "Child actors will only have to work four hours a day. They'll have to go to school, and be with other children. Have some kind of a normal life!" She shook her finger at Joey, but he didn't think she looked mean anymore. He liked what she was saying.

"That time will come, you'll see," she continued. "Someday you'll have a voice in your own future, young man."

Joey looked forward to that day. But meanwhile, the director was calling him. They were ready for him on the set. Slowly he got to his feet and went into the dark studio.

He stood on the deck of a pirate ship. It had been built just for the movie. A machine made the ship rock back and forth, as if it were really on the ocean. Joey got to carry a rubber knife and wear a patch over his eye. A long time ago, he would have thought all this was great, but now he was used to it. He yawned and wondered when he could eat lunch.

"*Pssst,*" he heard below him. Surprised, he looked down and saw a red-haired boy about his own age. The boy stood in the ship's hold, his finger to his lips. "I'm Chris," the boy said softly. "I play the stowaway."

Joey crouched so they could talk. Around him, people scurried this way and that, tilting the lights overhead, fixing the blue backdrop of the ocean.

"I found out where they're keeping the camels for the new desert picture," Chris whispered, "but I can't get the gate open by myself. Want to go over with me later? If no one's looking, I bet we could ride them . . ."

"Okay, places, everyone. Joey, let's go, please," the director called. "Camera rolling . . . interlock mike . . ."

*Camel riding!* Joey thought. But what about the movie? He was supposed to shoot a big scene later.

All of a sudden, he decided he'd speak up. He'd tell the director he needed a rest this afternoon. He hadn't had a day off in a long, long time.

*Camel riding!* he marveled again. You couldn't do *that* in the "outside World"!

"It's a deal," he said loudly to Chris, and grinned.

# ABOUT THIS BOOK

Much of this book—although it is fiction—is based on fact. For instance, it's true that, during the silent era, movies were very often made up as the shooting went along. And it's sad to think that sometimes, to get a child to cry for a scene, a director would tell terrible lies, as in the book when Joey is told his friend has been buried in a mudslide. But sometimes the facts are funny, too. At the American Biograph Studio in 1926, sheep really were placed on a high platform so they wouldn't wander out of camera range.

In 1927, the year this book takes place, America was heading into a difficult time. The Depression was just around the corner. People lost their jobs, and day-to-day life was grim. Still, many people would spend the few pennies they had not on food or rent, but on a ticket to the movies. They wanted to forget real life for a while, and escape to a more glamorous world, and they thought that world was Hollywood.

The Depression happened about the same time sound came to motion pictures. When I was researching this book, I watched many silent films, and then the first "talkie": *The Jazz Singer*. Try to imagine how amazed an audience must have been to hear someone talk in a movie for the first time. But Hollywood wasn't all glamour and magic. An actor whose voice wasn't right for talkies soon joined the millions of people across America without jobs.

In the late 1920s, child stars were the country's favorites. Sweet-faced child actors came to stand for the future, for a time when maybe life wouldn't be so hard. Often supporting an entire family, these children, like Joey, had to grow up very fast. When their voices changed, or when they got older and were no longer "cute," they, too, lost their jobs.

How strange it is that during an age when children of the screen were so adored, they were also used so unfairly. Laws about tutors and working hours for children existed but were rarely enforced. Across America, child labor meant cheap labor. It wasn't until 1938 that the Federal Labor Standards Act was passed and finally things really began to change.

In *Child Star*, I've tried to show a different side of the Depression. Adults needed to dream during those bad times; they needed escape and fantasy. In this case, it was children who helped them forget their troubles. Sometimes it was children who had to pay the price.

—L.W.